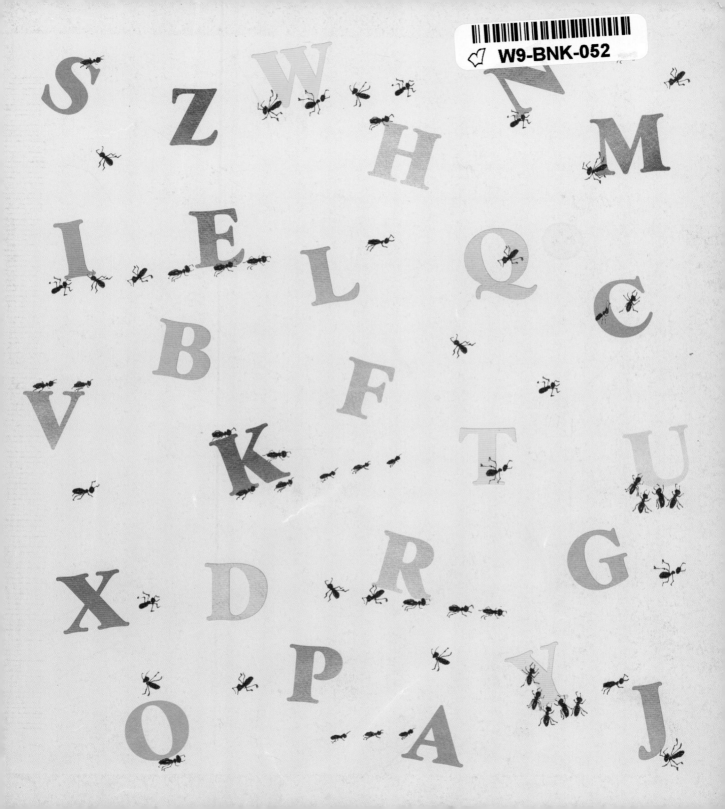

MAX's ABC

ROSEMARY WELLS

VIKING

VIKING
Published by Penguin Group
Penguin Young Readers Group, 345 Hudson Street, New York, New York 10014, U.S.A.
Penguin Group (Canada), 90 Eglinton Avenue East, Suite 700, Toronto, Ontario, Canada M4P 2Y3
(a division of Pearson Penguin Canada Inc.)
Penguin Books Ltd, 80 Strand, London WC2R 0RL, England
Penguin Ireland, 25 St Stephen's Green, Dublin 2, Ireland (a division of Penguin Books Ltd)
Penguin Group (Australia), 250 Camberwell Road, Camberwell, Victoria 3124, Australia
(a division of Pearson Australia Group Pty Ltd)
Penguin Books India Pvt Ltd, 11 Community Centre, Panchsheel Park, New Delhi – 110 017, India
Penguin Group (NZ), Cnr Airborne and Rosedale Roads, Albany, Auckland 1310, New Zealand
(a division of Pearson New Zealand Ltd)
Penguin Books (South Africa) (Pty) Ltd, 24 Sturdee Avenue, Rosebank, Johannesburg 2196, South Africa

Penguin Books Ltd, Registered Offices: 80 Strand, London WC2R 0RL, England

First published in 2006 by Viking, a division of Penguin Young Readers Group

1 3 5 7 9 10 8 6 4 2

Copyright © Rosemary Wells, 2006
All rights reserved

LIBRARY OF CONGRESS CATALOGING-IN-PUBLICATION DATA IS AVAILABLE

ISBN: 0-670-06074-7

Specica Markets ISBN 978-0-670-06247-8 Not for Resale

Manufactured in China
Set in Minister

This Imagination Library edition is published by Penguin Group (USA), a Pearson company,
exclusively for Dolly Parton's Imagination Library, a not-for-profit program designed
to inspire a love of reading and learning, sponsored in part by The Dollywood Foundation.
Penguin's trade editions of this work are available wherever books are sold.

To the Twinkles

Max's **A**nts escaped from their **A**nt farm.
They went looking for Max's birthday cake.

Up Max's pants they climbed. ***B**ite **B**ite **B**ite* went the ants on the **B**irthday cake.

Max poured his **C**up of **C**ranberry juice onto the ants in his pants.

Down **D**own **D**own went the juice.
Delicious! The ants **D**rank it up.

"**EEE**eeeeek!" said Max's sister Ruby.

Max took his pants off **F**ast!
But the ants stayed behind on
Max having **F**un.

"**G**ive me those pants, Max," Ruby said.
"**G**o! **G**o! **G**o away, ants!"

"Put on your **H**appy-face pants, Max," said Ruby.
"The ants are **H**istory!"

But the ants found an **I**ce pop in Max's pocket.
"**I**tch! **I**tch! **I**tch!" said Max.

Max **J**umped into the bath.

The ants **J**umped into the bath, too.

Max **K**icked his feet.
But the ants **K**icked their feet, too.

The ants **L**oved the bath.
They **L**aughed and splashed.

"I am going to use **M**iss **M**arvella's **M**agic
Bath Salts on the ants," said Ruby.

Ruby knew the ants could **N**ever **N**ibble their way through the bath salts.

"One, two, three, it's Over for the ants, Max!" said Ruby.

But it wasn't over for the ants.
The bath salts just turned the ants **P**ink and **P**urple.
"I have another idea, Max," said Ruby.

"What?" said Max.

"Good **Q**uestion, Max," said Ruby.

"Keep very **Q**uiet in your chair."

Ruby found a jar of **R**ed **R**aspberry jelly.

S

"**S**it **S**till, Max," said Ruby.
"We are **S**marter than those ants."

Ruby made **T**oast in the **T**oaster.
She put jelly on the **T**oast.
Then Ruby made a **T**rail of crumbs.

The trail ended **U**nderneath Max's chair.
The ants followed the trail.

Ruby was waiting for them
with the **V**acuum cleaner.

Wooooo! **W**ent the vacuum cleaner.
It sucked up all the ants.

"Gone forever!" said Ruby.
"**X** marks the spots where the ants used to be!"

But inside the vacuum bag the ants were enjoying cake and toast. "**Y**um **Y**um **Y**um," said the ants. Max heard them.

Max shook the ants out of the bag.
Soon they were home, fast asleep: **ZZZZZ**!